"Oi – watch where you're going!"

I don't see the man until too late and dodge past him, almost stumbling. He's swearing, but I don't care. I have to get away.

"Check out Running Man!" jokes someone outside the Kebab House. Other people, standing on the pavement, start to laugh. No one tries to help me.

Like every other Friday evening, the High Street is packed. Loads of blokes are gathered outside the mosque at the bottom of the road, enjoying the warm weather. The dome shimmers in the late sunshine.

A gang of teenage girls stand on the corner of Draper Street, all short skirts and bright make-up. Ordinarily I'd look again, but I have to keep going. No time to admire the scenery. The lads who are after me won't stop. They want my blood. They're animals …

An African man glares at me, as I barge him out of the way. I shout an apology and keep going. I run between two parked cars and weave through the heavy traffic. I want to get far ahead of my hunters. I can lose them in the streets near my house. Is that stupid, leading them back to where I live?

Are you wondering who they are, the people chasing me?

Easy. They're my girlfriend's brothers …

2

Ria

Momo isn't making any sense. "They're gonna kill him!" he shouts down the phone.

"What?" I whisper back.

I'm in the bathroom, hiding from my dad. If he catches me chatting to a boy, I'm done for. Like, properly dead. My dad doesn't want me talking to boys. My dad doesn't want me to have a life. My dad is harsh.

"Joey!" shouts Momo, and I understand. I gulp down air. I feel a bit sick.

"Who's after Joey?" I ask Momo.

"You deaf?" he screams at me. "Your brothers!"

"You sure?" I whisper.

"Yeah! You want me to call the cops?"

"No – my dad can't find out!" I say urgently. "He'll kill me!"

"Your brothers might kill Joey first," says Momo.

I think about the kiss. Wonder who saw us together. Someone must have told my family. My stomach turns somersaults.

"I'll call you back," I tell Momo. "Just let me think."

Momo swears and cuts me off. I can hear my dad coming up the stairs.

"*Ria*?" he calls out. "What you doing, Ria?"

I flush the toilet and then run the tap on the basin. "In the loo!" I shout back.

"Oh," my dad says, his voice close now. "I thought I heard you talking to someone."

I open the door and he's standing right there. He looks suspicious.

"I'm going out," he tells me. "You lock the door, and stay inside, okay?"

I nod at him.

"Your brothers are out too," he adds. "You make the food for 9 o'clock. We'll be back by then. Not for me, though. I'm getting chicken."

"No problem," I say, looking at my feet.

"You behave," he warns me. "Good girls don't mess about. Okay?"

I nod slowly. Since my mum died, my dad and brothers have taken over my life. Like, it wasn't great before, but now? They watch everything I do, control me. It makes me so angry. See, except for school, I can't go out unless my brothers or dad are with me. I can't wear what I want. There's no make-up in my bedroom, no PC, Blu-ray player or TV. I can't even keep books at home. It's like being in prison.

At least it was. Until I met Joey …

3

Joey

I met Ria at school. Noticed her in Year 10. She was wearing trousers instead of a skirt, and looked really shy. The other lads ignored her. They wanted the mouthy girls, the ones who liked to flirt. I used to, until I saw Ria. Her eyes are pale brown and her skin is creamy. She has bright pink lips and never wears make-up. Pure, natural beauty.

The first time we chatted, she blushed about ten times. I told her she was pretty – I'm gifted like that. I can chat up any girl, any time. I'm no model, but I can make them laugh. And girls like that.

"I don't go out with boys," she said.

"Yeah, you do," I joked. "You were just waiting for the *right* boy. And here I am …"

* * *

A brick flies past my head – and I'm back in the present. I'm running along Park Road, up into Eastfields. These are my ends, and Ria's brothers know it. They know I can get away – disappear down a back-alley, jump a wall. My side is aching, and I'm out of breath. My lungs feel like they're on fire. I can't stop though.

I take a side street and see my escape. A car garage – the blue doors open. An old sports car, silver with gold rims, sits in the entrance, half on the road. Barry, the mechanic, knows my mum. I see him appear from the other side of the car. I stop and try to catch my breath.

"Barry," I pant. "N-n-need your help!"

"What?" he asks, looking all confused.

"In trouble!" I shout, hiding behind his door. "Lads – after me …"

Barry shakes his head. He's wearing a knitted hat, his huge dreadlocks crammed in beneath it.

"Nah, man!" he tells me. "Don't bring your trouble here!"

I shake my head. "Ain't my fault – they're chasing me!" I say.

I peek back down the street. A van pulls up at the T-junction. Mercedes – black, sitting on eighteen inch ebony alloys. *Their* van.

"No!"

Barry looks down the street too, sees the lads.

"Okay," he says, pushing me into his workshop. "There's a back entrance, into the yard."

"Yeah, I know," I tell him. "Thanks."

Barry's yard backs onto a supermarket loading bay. Once I jump the wall, I can call someone. The police or my cousin Darryl, who has a car.

"Why they after you?" he asks.

"I kissed their sister."

Barry shakes his head, half-smiling.

"You kissed their sister? You – a *white* boy?"

I nod.

"Man, you must have a death wish!" he laughs. "Best run!"

I smile and duck out of the door. I only kissed Ria once. Four months of talking and flirting and hiding from everyone. All that for one kiss. Thing is, it was worth the wait. Ria was worth the wait …

4
Ria

As soon as my father leaves, I call Momo. I've got a plan but it's dangerous.

"Call Darryl," I tell Momo. "We need his car."

"No time," Momo replies. "They'll get Joey!"

"No other choice!" I shout back.

I hear Momo swear. I wonder how my family know about Joey. I think back to that day, a week earlier. I stayed after school, pretending to do my homework in the library. It's the only way I can spend time with Joey. We can't walk down the street. Someone might see us and tell my family …

"Amira!" I shout.

"Who?" asks Momo.

I tell him about a girl from school.

"She saw Joey and me together," I tell him. "She fancies one of my brothers. It can't be anyone else."

Momo sighs.

"I told you to be careful," he says. "Told you not to mess with fire."

Momo isn't like my brothers. He doesn't think what they do is right. His dad is lovely, too – proper chilled out and always cracking jokes. I sometimes wonder why my dad is so different from his. Momo understands what I'm facing – he doesn't think what I've done is wrong.

"Just call Darryl," I tell him. "I'll meet you by the phone shop on Park Road. Fifteen minutes."

"What if they catch Joey before that?" asks Momo.

"They won't," I reply. "Joey's too smart for them."

I run to my bedroom. I'm praying that Joey can dodge them. I can't think about him getting caught …

I throw the few clothes I have into my schoolbag. Underwear, toothbrush, phone charger and money go in too. I look around my room. Think about the night my mum died. Wonder what she's thinking, whether she's watching me.

"I'm sorry," I whisper. "I can't stay here any more."

See, if my brothers know about Joey, then my dad will find out too. And he'll kill me. He's already promised me to some man I've never met. It's a family honour thing. It's what good girls like me do. Dad says it's what my mum would have wanted. Thing is – *I* don't want to. But my dad won't care about that. It's how he was brought up, I guess. He wants me and my brothers to follow the rules that he learned as a kid.

I have no choice now. I have to run …

5

JOEY

I'm hiding behind a skip in the supermarket yard now. I call Darryl. His phone goes straight to answer.

"Great!" I whisper, listening out for Ria's brothers.

I know Barry won't sell me out, but her brothers aren't stupid. They'll just carry on searching the streets. If I stay where I am, I can think up a plan. I'm three streets from home, but can't risk going there. If they know where I live, my mum might get hurt too. I've got to think …

I try Darryl again but still get no reply. I wonder where he is, why he isn't answering his phone. I text him – tell him what's going on. A small rat slopes past my feet, stopping to nibble at some mouldy bread. I stamp my foot and it scampers away.

I hear swearing and the sound of footsteps.

"Oi!" the supermarket manager shouts. He's a Sri Lankan man with yellow teeth. "Get out from there!"

"Ssh!" I whisper. "I'm hiding, mate. Some lads are after me!"

He shakes his head.

"You go or I call the police!" he warns. "This is private property!"

He shows me his phone, and I swear at him.

"Get out!" he shouts, threatening me with the broom that he's holding.

I shake my head. Can my day get any worse?

6

Ria

I think about leaving a note but what's the point?
Once I run, that's it. My dad will disown me.
My brothers will hunt for me. The shame will make
them forget that they love me. That I'm their baby
sister …

I try the front door, but it won't budge. That's
when I understand. It's locked from the outside.
My keys are missing too. My dad has taken them.
I feel sick.

"He already knows," I say to an empty house.

I'm in serious trouble. I *have* to get out. I go to
the kitchen, praying that he's forgotten the back
door keys. He hasn't. The utility room has a small
window that doesn't bolt properly. The other
windows will be secure, because they always are.

I reach across the washing machine and push the window open. It's small, but I should be able to squeeze through. I throw my backpack out first, and then climb onto the washing machine.

My heart is beating so fast, I think I might die. My tongue is dry and heavy in my mouth. I turn, and put one leg through. I take a deep breath, and then I'm in the garden.

I look around, trying to think. Our garden has no access to the street, but my neighbour's does. He's an old white guy called Keith and he's really lovely. When no one's watching, I chat to him about my life. After today, I probably won't ever see him again. The thought makes me very sad. His fence is only waist-high and from his garden, I can escape.

"Ria?" I hear him say.

He's standing in his narrow passageway. I step over the fence and approach him across his lawn.

"Are you okay, love?" he asks, eyeing my backpack. His hair is short and white, his eyes dark.

I shake my head. "They found out," I tell him.

"About Joey?"

I nod, and Keith gives me a big hug.

"Are you leaving then?" he adds.

I nod again. Tears stream down my face.

"I understand," he tells me. "Get out, child. Go and see the world. There's no sense in staying here."

Keith knows everything because I've told him. As a soldier, he travelled all round the world. He tells me stories about the Middle East and Singapore. Says that I deserve more than some husband I don't even know. Blink and it's gone, he once said to me. He was talking about Life.

"They'll ask if you saw me," I tell him, taking in the scent from his old jumper.

"Stuff 'em," he replies. "I was watching telly. I didn't see a thing."

He smiles and we walk into his kitchen. He grabs an old coffee container from a shelf.

"Got this in Brazil," he says. "Three times your age, this thing." He removes the lid and I see it's stuffed with cash.

"I don't need your money," I tell him, but he shakes his head.

"What are you going to live on, daft girl?" he asks. "Fresh air?"

He shoves about two hundred quid into my hands. Asks if I need a lift anywhere. I nod. "Park Road," I say.

"Is Joey going with you?" he asks.

I shrug. "I don't know," I tell him.

"I'll get my keys," he says.

7

Joey

Ria's mouth tasted like lemons and sugar when we kissed. My head was buzzing afterwards, too. It was like waiting for the best PlayStation game ever to come out, and then playing it for the first time. When I held her close, I could feel the heat from her body. I'd kissed plenty of girls before, but no one like her. She was special. She *is* special …

* * *

… I'm back on the street, by the supermarket entrance. Shoppers come and go. The manager is at the door, giving me dirty looks. I ignore him and check my phone. My battery is running low – down to fifteen per cent. It buzzes and I see Momo's name. I answer quickly.

"Where you at?" he asks.

"The Spar, up Evington Road," I tell him. "Did you call the cops?"

"Nah, bruv," he replies. "I called Ria first. She said to phone Darryl."

"I tried him," I tell Momo. "He didn't pick up."

"Don't worry – I'm with him now. We'll grab Ria, then get you."

I gulp at the mention of her name. What does he mean?

'"Ria?" I ask.

"Yeah," he tells me. "Ain't you spoken to her?"

I haven't got time to reply. I see the black Mercedes van screech to a stop opposite me. The doors fly open. One of Ria's brothers jumps out of the van, his face twisted with rage.

"You're dead, white boy!" he yells at me.

"Gotta run!" I shout, and I'm off again.

Two of her brothers chase me on foot. The other two drive. I sprint, desperate to get away. How stupid can I get? Standing in the open, chatting on the phone.

I curse myself, as I turn right. The road is packed, the cars stuck in a jam. I weave through them, heading for James Street. There are seven alleys that run off it. Seven ways to escape again. Only, I'm not watching my step, and I smack my right thigh against an iron bollard. My thigh goes numb and the pain makes my eyes water. Dead leg …

I'm stumbling now, not running, and they're gaining on me. I'm going the wrong way, too. My friends are in the opposite direction. I need to find them. But that means going back on myself, which is a stupid idea. Only, if I don't go back, I'll get caught for sure.

And then I'm dead …

8

Ria

Momo and Darryl are waiting on Park Road. I jump straight into the car and we drive off.

"Where's Joey?" I ask.

"He was up by the Spar," Momo tells me. "Then we got cut off."

I want to cry. I'm scared for Joey.

"Why?" I ask.

Momo shrugs.

"Don't worry," he replies. "Joey will be okay."

But he gives Darryl a concerned look, and I know he's lying to me.

Darryl stays silent, concentrating on the road. He's eighteen, two years older than the rest of us.

"Are we going past the supermarket?" I ask.

"Guess so," says Darryl. "Try calling him again."

I pull out my phone, see that the battery is almost dead, and shake my head.

"My battery's too low," I tell him. "And I'm going to need it later."

"I'll call him," says Momo.

Only Joey doesn't answer, and I start to get really scared. Like, what if my brothers have got him?

At the supermarket, the manager is by the door. Joey isn't there. Darryl pulls up to the kerb and Momo gets out. He talks to the manager. I can't hear them, even with the window down. There's too much noise from cars and people, and I can hear a reggae tune blasting out from somewhere.

Momo looks angry and shouts at the man. Then he stomps back to the car.

"Manager said he caught Joey hiding in the back yard," Momo tells us. "But he told him to go away."

"Were they after him?" I ask, talking about my brothers.

This time Momo doesn't lie to me.

"Yeah," he tells me.

I gulp down air as Momo tries Joey's phone again.

"What's the bag for?" asks Darryl, looking at me in the rear-view mirror.

I shrug.

"Can't go back home now," I say.

9

Joey

I'm in a bad way. My leg feels numb and my lungs are burning. I'm stumbling down an alley, with brick walls on either side. It's dark and narrow, and the floor is wet. I don't know where I'm going. It's like my brain has frozen. I just want to get away. I want Ria …

* * *

She told me all about herself. About her mum dying and her dad being strict. She explained that her brothers were dangerous – that we had to hide. She even told me about the man in her dad's village, back in his old country. Some farmer who wants a British-born wife. Ria said she would be forced to marry him – to make him food and babies, and never go out.

I told her that it sounded like hell, and she agreed.

"But," she said, "that's what I'm expected to do."

"And if you don't?" I asked her.

But Ria just smiled at me, hiding the truth.
I could just have dumped her – found a girl
without all the stress attached. Only, Ria wasn't just
some girl. She was the first one that I *really* liked –
know what I mean?

* * *

Ria's family are gaining on me. I can hear their
trainers thudding against the ground. Then I see my
mistake. I've taken the wrong alley. It's a dead end.

"NO!" I shout. I swear her brothers are laughing
at me. I can't see them but I can imagine their faces.

There's no choice. I grab the top of the wall,
drag myself up. I have no idea what's on the other
side, and no time to check.

I get over and land on some metal bins. My legs buckle underneath me and I smack my face against the bricks.

It feels like fireworks are exploding in my head and body. I yell in pain but manage to steady myself again. I've given myself a chance now.

I hide in a corner, taking in air, with no idea which shop I'm behind. I just know that I'm parallel with the main road.

I get an idea, and think. Twenty shops lie between me and my destination – twenty yards or gardens for me to get past.

As I think, my phone vibrates in my pocket …

10

Ria

When I told Joey why I'd never had a boyfriend, he just sat and listened. He could have picked some other girl. Someone easier to go out with. Girls who were allowed into town, and on dates. Girls who didn't make him wait four months for a *kiss*.

"You're different," he told me.

"You're mad," I replied.

"Nah, seriously, Ria," he said. "You're like a red diamond. Other diamonds come and go, but a red one is the rarest …"

I remember wondering how he knew that, and why. And then I realised I didn't care. I just wanted to kiss him.

* * *

I grab the phone from Momo.

"Where are you, babe?"

Joey sounds breathless when he replies.

"In some yard, behind James Street," he pants. "You okay?"

"Yeah – I'm with Momo and Darryl."

"Won't you get into trouble?"

"Yeah," I tell him. "But I don't care any more."

"Your brothers are proper angry," he says.

"Don't let them catch you," I warn. "Seriously, Joey. They'll kill you."

Joey gives me a little laugh.

"I worked that out," he jokes.

"Babe, be serious!"

"Tell Darryl to drive to the end of Buckingham Road, you know, where the Maryland Fried Chicken is?"

I tell him that I know it. Everyone knows Maryland.

"Wait by the front door and keep the engine running. I'll be there in ten minutes."

"Okay. Hurry, yeah?" I say.

"Only if you promise me a kiss," he replies.

"You can have fifty," I tell him. "Just don't get caught."

11

JOEY

I hop walls, through gardens and yards, all the way to Buckingham Road. It's hard going. My jeans are torn, my leg is throbbing, and my chest feels like it's collapsing.

Two of the brothers are still behind me. They're shouting and yelling. I know that they're getting tired too. The other two are probably on the main road, watching out for me.

Thing is, I've got a plan. If I can get into the yard behind Maryland, I'll be fine. They always leave their back door open. Instead of taking the street, I can go through the shop. Meet my mates out front. Ria's brothers won't expect me to come out that way.

The sun is going down now, and the air is warm and humid. Sweat is running down my back and chest, and my legs feel clammy. My hunters are two or three gardens behind me, but they *are* catching up. I've got maybe three more walls to jump over.

I take another huge breath and go again …

12

Ria

It's only when we pull up outside Maryland Fried Chicken that I realise …

It's Friday night, and the shop is packed with customers – mostly men. Some youths, about fourteen years old, are standing on the pavement by the door. They're local lads, just hanging out. That's what the lads round my way do.

Most of them are Asian, but there are some others too. Joey knows some of them. The problem isn't the young lads though …

The problem is …

13

JOEY

Maryland's back door is wide open. The yard
is filled with empty boxes and bags of rubbish.
I pounce off the wall and almost crash into one
of the workers. He's carrying two bin liners and
looks startled.

"Sorry, bruv!" I call out. "Gotta get going …"

I run past him, into the heat of the shop. Three
huge fryers sit to my left, and a grill to the right.
I weave past two more workers, to the counter
out front. The workers are shouting now, and they
don't look pleased, but I don't care. I ignore the
customers too – the shop is packed with them.
All I see is Darryl's dodgy old Ford Focus – dark
metallic blue with a 1.6 litre engine and scuffed
wheels. My chariot awaits me …

I duck under the counter and run into some lads from my school.

"Watch it!" shouts one of them, some Asian brother with a bad boy scowl. I shove past and see some more people I know. One of them grins.

"You sweating, bro?" he jokes, as I hear Ria's brothers crash into the shop behind me.

I push past more customers, older Asian men giving me dirty looks, and reach the door. I can see Darryl at the wheel of his car. I can see Ria in the back. I give her a huge smile.

I step out, and then I see the Mercedes van pull up across the street.

"Open the door!" I shout, as my world shrinks. There are two men behind me, and two in front. My life is now just fifty yards of action. Make the car, escape and live. Get caught, fall to the pavement. Die …

14

Ria

I see Joey emerge from the shop. He spots me and grins like an idiot. I'm already opening the door …

"Joey!" shouts Momo from the front. "The van!"

Two of my brothers have pulled up across the street. My throat goes dry.

"Hurry up!" yells Darryl.

They're closing in on Joey from in front, and he tries to turn. But then I see my dad coming up behind him. Joey's trapped. Dad's face twists with rage. He grabs Joey from behind. Joey falls …

I scream out and feel my legs start to tremble.

"JOEY!!!" Momo yells, as I hear police sirens approaching.

My dad sees me in the car and lunges forward. Two of my brothers run out of the shop. They look like wolves on the hunt …

Then the car screeches away, and it's all gone. I puke into my lap and pass out …

As one of Ria's brothers stands over me, I hear the police cars coming. I try to look up, but there's too much pain. I can't see Ria's face, no matter how much I want to. But I *do* hear Darryl drive off, and I smile inside. I don't want Ria to be here. Don't want her to get caught too.

The brother leans over me, spits in my face.

"Dirty, stinking ..."

His words fade away as I think about the kiss. It was supposed to be the first kiss of many ...

The one that made Ria mine ...

It wasn't meant to lead to *this* ...

Reader challenge

Word hunt

 On page 4, find a verb that means "glimmers" or "sparkles".

 On page 21, find a verb that means "abandon" or "reject".

 On page 44, find two adjectives that mean "damp" or "sweaty".

Story sense

 Why does Ria lie to her dad about being on the phone? (page 7)

 What does Barry mean when he says to Joey, "Man, you must have a death wish"? (page 14)

 How are Momo and his dad different from Ria's family? (page 16)

 How do you think Ria is feeling as they pull up outside Maryland Fried Chicken? (page 45)

 At the end of the story, why do you think Joey focuses his mind on the kiss? (page 53)

Your views

9. Do you think it was a good plan for Ria to run away from home? Give reasons.

10. What do you think happened to Joey at the end of the story? Give reasons.

Spell it

With a partner, look at these words and then cover them up.

- expected

- exploding

- explained

Take it in turns for one of you to read the words aloud. The other person has to try and spell each word. Check your answers, then swap over.

Try it

With a partner, imagine you are Joey and Ria. Act out a brief telephone conversation just before Joey gets caught. Look at pages 39 to 41 to help you plan what you will say to each other.

William Collins's dream of knowledge for all began with the publication of his first book in 1819. A self-educated mill worker, he not only enriched millions of lives, but also founded a flourishing publishing house. Today, staying true to this spirit, Collins books are packed with inspiration, innovation and practical expertise. They place you at the centre of a world of possibility and give you exactly what you need to explore it.

Collins. Freedom to teach.

Published by Collins Education
An imprint of HarperCollins*Publishers*
77-85 Fulham Palace Road
Hammersmith
London
W6 8JB

Browse the complete Collins Education catalogue at **www.collins.co.uk**

Text © Bali Rai 2014
Illustrations © Chris Coady 2014

Series consultants: Alan Gibbons and Natalie Packer

10 9 8 7 6 5 4 3 2 1
ISBN 978-0-00-746487-6

British Library Cataloguing in Publication Data.
A catalogue record for this publication is available from the British Library.

Commissioned by Catherine Martin
Edited by Sue Chapple
Project-managed by Lucy Hobbs and Caroline Green
Illustration management by Tim Satterthwaite
Proofread by Hugh Hillyard-Parker
Typeset by Jouve India, Ltd
Production by Emma Roberts
Printed and bound in China by South China Printing Co.
Cover design by Paul Manning

Acknowledgements

The publishers would like to thank the students and teachers of the following schools for their help in trialling the *Read On* series:

Parkview School, London
Queensbury School, Queensbury, Bradford
Southfields Academy, London
St Mary's College, Hull
Westergate Community School, Chichester